Life Of The Party

A Christmas Novella

by

Jay W. Foreman

Copyright © 2020 by Jay W. Foreman

Special Thanks to:

Doug Palmer for graphic design, cover artwork, formatting, and about a hundred more things that were completely over my head.

Vicki Lewis for editing and making me look much more grammatically proficient than I actually am.

Introduction

I originally wrote this story in 2009 as a script for a Christmas play for Grace Community Church in Winchester, Virginia. I truly believe the story was God-inspired because I was able to write it in its entirety in one afternoon, not knowing how it would end until I actually arrived at the ending. It was a lot of fun as a live production and brought together a wonderful cast of characters that gave everything they had to make this a huge success. Even an ice storm on opening night didn't keep folks away.

My goal for turning the script into a novella was to remind everyone that we are always part of God's greater plan. We are never outside of His love or grace. Even when we feel like we're drifting, God remains diligent in guiding our footsteps.

I hope you enjoy the following tale. I hope
you laugh. I hope you reflect. And I hope you
appreciate how loved you are.

Thank you for buying this book and
helping me put my daughter through college!

Jay

Foreword

"I'm going ALL IN."   Van McNeely — Life of the Party

When Jay asked me to write the foreword for Life of the Party, I was honored beyond words. When he shared with me that he was turning his hit story for the stage into a book, I knew immediately what that meant. It meant that the world now gets to read and experience what Life Of The Party is all about. On a personal note, I was blessed enough to act in the live production of the play, on stage, as the infamous character, Van McNeely.

This book personifies what it means to go 'all in' in life, love, family, and faith. Jay has genuinely captured lightning in a bottle by sharing the story of each character in this book, the timeless lessons they learn, much to their surprise, and then tying them all together.

Life Of The Party has impacted me in a way that I never thought possible. It opened my eyes to what can happen if you are open to seeing what is in front of you. The greatest gift we are given is the time we are offered to share our life, love, and friendship with others. As we all know, we are a part of God's plan, not our plan, and Life Of The Party teaches us that we need to cherish the time we have with each other.

As a reader, if you can remember a moment in time, be it an event, production, play, school class, or social gathering, where God put a unique and fun group of people together, just for a short time, and never together again, that was the live production of Life Of The Party.

Jay has taken this amazing story, made it come to life, and now he is sharing it with you on the following pages of this book.

I encourage you to open your eyes and your heart to this story; it may just surprise you.

Godspeed and enjoy.

Danny Argiro — *Author, Speaker, Entrepreneur, and, of course, Van McNeely.*

Chapter 1

Howard Mudd stood by the food table sampling different cheeses. He wasn't a big fan of cheese, but it was one of only a few appetizers he recognized. Someone had encouraged him to try the boursin, and after doing so, he realized he preferred Kraft singles. He continued to fidget in his coat and tie, which was not his everyday attire. Earlier in the evening, he had tested the theory that tying a tie was like riding a bike…once you do it, you never forget. It took him a few tries to get the tie length where he wanted it, but he managed. His sport coat was making him uncomfortable as well. He couldn't remember the last time he had worn it, but could have sworn that his wife, Molly, must have shrunk it in the wash since then.

He watched the other partygoers talk and laugh and show off for one another as Brenda Lee's, *Rockin' Around the Christmas Tree,* played in the background. Howard liked a lot of things about Christmas, but Van McNeely's annual Christmas party was not one of them. Yet every year, despite his protests, he ended up back here again. Molly really enjoyed these gatherings, so in the spirit of trying to be a good husband, Howard's refusals were typically not too emphatic.

This year's party was harder to get psyched up for than in years past. Howard had a lot on his mind with nobody to talk with about it. Various pressures from different areas of his life had been closing in like a vice lately, and he didn't have any answers or even any outlets. Howard didn't have an ego and was content to live a simple life, but was feeling lately like he was somewhat toxic and that those around him deserved better than what he had to offer in whatever role he happened to play.

Howard realized he needed to stop spending so much time alone with his thoughts, so he scouted the room for his friend, Bryan Fletcher. Besides Molly and their daughter, Heather, he was the only other person at the party with whom he felt like talking. He was trying to find Bryan, but at the same time trying not to make direct eye contact with anyone else out of fear that he would end up having to exchange mindless pleasantries. Howard had already spent more time than he would have liked making small talk with a pompous young man that had to have been fifteen years younger.

All Howard took away from the much-too-long, one-sided conversation was that the man had some kind of job managing other people's finances. He kept dropping words like *bond, yield, index,* and *call.* Maybe the guy made sense, but Howard was only half paying attention. He finally guzzled the rest of his drink just to have an excuse to get a refill and end his misery.

Avoiding people and trying to find Bryan was no small task. The room they were in was astronomical. Van called it his Great Room. *Really?* Howard thought to himself. *Who has a Great Room these days?* But despite Howard's annoyance with Van's pompousness, he couldn't help but be impressed with the room itself. He wasn't sure, but was pretty confident he could fit his entire house in this one room. As if that weren't enough, the raised ceilings and stained mahogany arches made the room feel even larger than it actually was. There was more marble than Howard had ever seen in one place and paintings on the wall that, while they did nothing for him, had to be considered fine art.

All of the decor appeared so sterile that Howard wondered if Van even entered this room except for special occasions like this party. Not using this room could be easily done, seeing as how the mansion was over twelve thousand square feet, not including the guesthouse in back on one of his twenty-two rolling acres of his spacious Maryland suburb. As a feeling of inadequacy started to sweep over Howard, he caught a glimpse of Molly's shoulder-length auburn red hair out of the corner of his eye. She was heading his way carrying two drinks.

"Smile, Howard. You're at a party, remember?" she said, grinning, as she handed him one of the drinks.

"How could I forget? I'm surrounded by crappy food, phony people, and cheesy Christmas music," replied Howard, not returning Molly's smile.

"Well then, Mr. Scrooge, I'll just have to have enough fun for the both of us." Molly smiled a genuine smile and toasted the statement by clinking her long-stemmed glass of white wine with Howard's highball glass of tonic water.

"You do that."

"I will. After all, this party was an excuse for me to buy this new dress, and you haven't said a word about it yet." Molly spun around with her arms out by her sides to show off her new outfit, with her smile even bigger now. The black cocktail dress fanned out and lifted slightly above her knees as she twirled. "So? What do you think?"

"How much did it cost?" asked Howard, stoically.

"Ugghh! Don't worry. I got it off of the sale rack," replied Molly.

"No. I'm serious," continued Howard. "You know money gets tight around this time of year. How much did it cost?" Howard suddenly realized that Molly's answer would have to wait. As if his night wasn't already painful enough, here came none other than the party host himself, Van McNeely.

Chapter 2

Van took his time approaching the couple. This was a common trait of Van's. He was deliberately unhurried in anything he did, as if to show that his time was more important than anyone else's. Even his speech was slow and methodic, tempting Howard to always want to jump in and interrupt. He wasn't sure if this was because he wasn't speaking fast enough or because he didn't care to hear about Van's usual topic of conversation…*himself.*

Van was wearing charcoal gray slacks with a navy-blue jacket that Howard was sure he hadn't purchased off the rack. It's not that it fit that nice, but he knew that wasn't Van's style. *Heck, it's probably not even made in America!* Van was known for his international shopping excursions. Clothes, cars, even real estate. Howard guessed that the hair gel he used to grease back his salt-and-pepper hair was imported as well. Under Van's sport coat, he wore an even more annoying white turtleneck with a gaudy oversized gold chain hanging around his neck. Howard thought that look had long since been out of style. *But I guess if you're rich, you make your own style.*

"Howard. Molly. Thank you both so much for coming," he said as he took Molly's hand and kissed the back of it…a little too long for Howard's liking.

"Are you kidding, Van? We wouldn't dream of missing your annual Christmas party. You always do such a fantastic job of hosting," Molly returned.

"Thank you, Molly. As always, you're much too kind to me." Van then held up his glass of champagne and gestured to the room in general. "Sure, it costs me a small fortune each year, but hey, for good friends…it's worth it."

Van then turned the conversation to Howard, but never took his eyes off of Molly. "Howard, have you tried the pâté yet?"

"Pâté?" asked Howard, doing his best to show that he was not impressed.

"Yes," replied Van, finally turning his attention to Howard. "It's a delightful delicacy. I serve it every year, but this year I've outdone myself again. I just can't help myself. This year's pâté is made with goose liver. I had it imported. You must try some. It's to die for."

"I believe you," said Howard. "Because I'd rather die than put goose liver in my mouth."

Molly flushed a light shade of red from embarrassment. "Forgive him. His appreciation of appetizers ends with Vienna Sausages," she said to Van, trying to diffuse the situation.

Van forced a polite laugh for Molly's sake. He then snapped his fingers for a waiter to bring over the tray of appetizers he had mentioned. "I assure you, Howard, this will be much more enjoyable than anything you eat from a pop-top can. Life is about trying new things. Not being so stuck in your ways."

Howard rolled his eyes. The only thing less enjoyable than being at Van's party was to actually be given life lessons by him. A moment later, one of the floating waiters dressed in a traditional black-and-white tuxedo, answered Van's summons. As he got closer to Van and the couple, it became blatantly apparent that his mouth was full. Van looked furious. Howard couldn't help but smile. *Maybe this party would offer up some entertainment after all.*

Chapter 3

"Yes, sir," began the waiter. "You called?" His voice was garbled by whatever food he had in his mouth. He was desperately trying to finish chewing.

Van stared at him in disbelief. "Are...are you eating my appetizers?" he asked.

With one hand supporting a platter full of hors d'oeuvres, the waiter held up his free hand's index finger to Van, as if to say, *Wait just a moment while I finish chewing my food.* Howard smiled and was curious to see how this was going to unfold. He doubted Van was used to this kind of treatment. *Especially by the hired help. Especially by someone that looked so out of place at this stuffy shindig. He looked like a surfer from the West Coast.* At least this is what Howard thought a California surfer would look like. Indiana was as far as he'd ever ventured from the East Coast. The waiter had dirty blonde hair parted down the middle, and Howard noticed he had a habit of constantly running his fingers through his bangs, trying to push his hair out of his dimly lit eyes.

The waiter finally swallowed and then spoke. "Instead of eating your food, sir, I'd like to refer to what just happened here as...quality control. I'm simply making sure the food is up to your usual high standard of excellence." He then smiled at Van, as if his explanation would square things between them.

Van took his time, as he always did. He sized up the server from top to bottom and then bottom to top. He regained his composure and then returned the smile. "You're new to the wait staff, aren't you?" he asked.

"Yes, sir."

"What's your name?"

"Chuck."

"Well, Chuck, I'm sure my food is excellent. Consider what's in your mouth your last bite. Are we clear?"

"Crystal, sir."

"Good. Now please offer some of the goose liver pâté you're holding to my friends," Van commanded.

Chuck's dull eyes suddenly brightened and grew to the size of silver dollars. He nervously shifted glances from Howard and Molly back to Van. "This is…I just ate…goose liver?" he asked to nobody in particular. "Oh! I think I'm going to be sick!" He handed his platter off to Molly and started to dry heave.

"Get a hold of yourself, man!" threatened Van.

"Which way is the bathroom? I'm going to be sick," said Chuck. His face was already turning a pale shade of green.

"Down the hall and to your right," said Van, as Chuck took off sprinting in that direction. He bumped into a few guests as he fled.

"Forgive that display," Van continued, as he took the food platter from Molly. "If you'll excuse me, I need to go mingle. But don't go far. We need to catch up some more." Again, he focused his stare on Molly and not Howard.

Chapter 4

Van was scarcely out of earshot before the mocking commenced. Howard twirled around with his arms out, as if to call attention to the room itself. *"Sure, it costs me a small fortune…have you tried the goose liver? It's imported,"* he said in a high-pitched voice with an accent that Molly wasn't sure was English or Australian.

She was not amused by his immaturity. "Okay. First of all, quit making fun of Van. Second of all, *what* kind of accent is that supposed to be?" Molly asked, arms folded across her chest, leaning on her back leg.

"You know, like a *rich person* accent," Howard replied.

"You're an idiot," said Molly, trying to diffuse the situation. It's just Van being Van. You need to let it go."

"Well, it doesn't help with you egging him on like you do." Then Howard dramatically threw his arms up in the air and broke into his high-pitched indecipherable accent again. "*We wouldn't dream of missing your annual Christmas party, Van. You always do such a fantastic job of hosting,*" he said, ending in an overexaggerated curtsy.

Molly was indifferent as she watched Howard's theatrics. "Okay. Is that the same *rich person* accent or a new one? Because they sound exactly the same."

"I'm just sick of seeing that guy flaunt his money around," said Howard. Then he raised his voice and shouted over in Van's direction. "We get it, Van! You're filthy rich!"

"Get a hold of yourself, Howard," said Molly, as she grabbed his arm and spun them both in the opposite direction of Van. "You're still not upset that Van and I used to date, are you?"

"Are *you*?" Howard fired back.

"What's that supposed to mean?"

"It means I'm sure if you were married to Van, you wouldn't have to buy your dresses off of the sale rack."

"Listen," said Molly calmly, trying to reel in the conversation. "I love you. That's why I married you." She then put both hands on Howard's shoulders and looked him in the eyes. "But right now…you're acting crazy. I'm going to go mingle. I suggest you take a deep breath, relax, and do the same."

Howard rolled his eyes. "Oh, and be nice to Kevin when he arrives," said Molly.

"Who's Kevin?" asked Howard.

"Very funny," said Molly, releasing her husband's shoulders. "He should be here any time to pick up Heather for their date. Behave!"

"Remind me again. Do we like Kevin?" asked Howard.

"He seems like a nice guy," said Molly.

"You say that about everyone," said Howard.

"Well, that's because there's good in everyone," Molly stated, defending her stance. "Besides, Heather met him during an outreach program at church. That shows he has some good intentions."

Howard laughed. "Yeah, and the only reason he was part of a church outreach program is that his intentions were to ask out our daughter!"

"And you know this, how?" asked Molly.

"Because he's a *guy*!" Howard replied. "That means he's a pig."

"You're a guy," stated Molly. "Does that mean you're a pig, too?"

"We're all pigs," said Howard. "Some of us just aren't as muddy as others."

"Okay. I don't even want to know what that means. And now I'm officially bored with this conversation." She started to walk away and turned around, flashing her gorgeous smile one more time. "I love you."

"You, too," said Howard, staring down at his drink.

Chapter 5

A few moments later, Chuck walked out of the bathroom. He was at the end of a corridor decorated with contemporary paintings. Each painting was perfectly spaced from the next, giving off more of a museum bareness rather than a home's warmth. Most paintings were abstract, showcasing various pastel colors, which really popped against the deep, rich wallpaper. The color was streaming back to Chuck's face as he wiped his hands with a towel.

"Excuse me! Chuck, is it?" called Van. He was walking toward him, again in no hurry. This time, Van was carrying with him a leather-bound binder.

"Yes, sir," replied Chuck, snapping to attention as if he were addressing a commanding officer in the military.

Van approached Chuck and opened the binder. He then pulled out a pair of reading glasses from his coat pocket and placed them on the end of his nose. "I'm looking at the catering list, and I don't see your name on here anywhere. Do you care to explain that?"

"Oh, yes, sir," said Chuck. "You see, there was a last-minute cancellation. One of our guys got sick or something, and I was called to fill in. I have my paperwork right here." Chuck reached into his pants pocket and fished around for a few seconds. After coming up empty, he checked his other pants pocket. A moment later, he pulled out a wadded-up piece of paper. After picking a few pieces of lent off of it, he uncrumpled it the best he could and handed it to Van.

Van took his time as he peered down at the paper through his glasses that were so far down his nose that they looked like they could fall off at any moment. "Okay. I guess you check out after all. But, I don't think serving food is a very good fit for you. Why don't you take over handling the music for this evening?"

"It would be an honor, sir," said Chuck, standing at attention and giving Van a mock salute.

Van didn't even acknowledge the gesture. "It's an easy job. Everything is digital. Just keep an eye on the playlists on the screen behind the sound system. The holiday playlists are clearly marked. The rules are simple. I don't want any songs repeated throughout this evening, and I certainly don't want any dead air. Continuous music with no repeats. Do you think you can handle that?"

"Absolutely," replied Chuck, with a smile. "Just tell me again where you said the cassette tapes were." Van stared back, either not getting the joke or clearly not amused by it. "Kidding! Bad joke, Van…er, Mr. McNeely. Consider it handled. Now go enjoy your party."

Chuck walked away to take over music duty. "Wrong way," Van called back, as he pinched the bridge of his nose with his thumb and index finger. He was starting to develop a headache, and he knew just who was responsible.

"Thanks!" Chuck called back. He gave Van a thumbs-up followed by a mischievous grin and started in the opposite direction.

Chapter 6

Howard had not moved from his previous spot and was nursing the tonic water that Molly had brought him earlier. Out of nowhere came a hearty slap on the back, nearly causing him to drop his drink. He spun around to see none other than his best friend, Bryan Fletcher. He was surprised he hadn't noticed him before. In a room full of guests all decked out in drab jackets and ties and cocktail dresses, Bryan definitely stood out in his electric-orange Hawaiian shirt, blue jeans, Converse high-tops, and Santa Claus hat.

Bryan never dressed up for Van's parties, and Howard knew it infuriated Van. He wondered why Van even invited Bryan year after year. Then he figured that Van was smart enough to realize that even if Bryan didn't get an invitation, he'd probably just crash it anyway. Howard figured the only reason that either one of them received invites was that they had all known each other since school when they were younger, and this was one of Van's ways of showing everyone just how much better off he had turned out.

"What's happening, Howie?" asked Bryan in a booming voice. He was shorter and skinnier than Howard, but always made up for it with the size of his presence in a room.

"Hey, Bryan," Howard returned, shaking his hand. "Where are Kelli and Natalie?"

Howard looked around to see if he saw Bryan's wife or daughter.

"Natalie came down with the flu, so Kelli's home taking care of her," he said, as he took a generous gulp of his iced tea.

"Sorry to hear that. Do you guys need anything?" asked Howard.

"Nah…we're all good. Thanks for asking. I swung by the store and loaded up on soup and crackers and medicine for her. I'm also going to cut out of here a little early tonight just to make sure they're okay. I wasn't even going to come, but Kelli insisted, since we RSVP'd. I argued that Van wouldn't care either way, but here I am. Like I'd rather spend my evening with a guy like Van McNeely than my own family. That'll be the day," replied Bryan.

He then looked around the room and back at Howard. "How about the spread this year? Can you believe it? I think ol' Van has outdone himself again. Did you know that there's an ice sculpture of Rudolph in the dining room? An ice sculpture, dude! That's crazy!" Then he motioned Howard to move closer and lowered his voice. "Look, don't tell anyone," Bryan said as moved his drink toward Howard. "I broke off Rudolph's nose to use as an ice cube." He then burst out laughing as if he had just delivered the funniest punch line that anyone in the history of the world had ever heard.

"Nice," Howard said, vaguely smiling.

"What's with you, man?" Bryan asked. "It's Christmas! It's a party! It's a *Christmas Party*! Life does not *get* any better than this!"

"How can you be in such a good mood after what happened at work today?" asked Howard.

And there it was. Howard verbally addressed one of the issues that was eating away at him.

"Is that what's bothering you? What happened at work today? Let it go, man. They're discretionary…not guaranteed. So what if we didn't get our Christmas bonuses this year?" Then he elbowed Howard in the ribs. "At least we still have our good looks, right?"

Howard was unfazed by Bryan's attempt at levity. "I know they're not guaranteed. But it's not like they didn't give out bonuses *period*. A lot of folks' paychecks were a lot fatter today."

"I know," answered Bryan. "And ours could have been, too, if we had worked a little more overtime."

"What's that supposed to mean?" snapped Howard.

"Nothing."

"I guess it's my fault that you didn't get your bonus, either?" Howard continued.

Bryan took a ceremonial step backward. "That's not even close to what I said. Look, I have no regrets over the choices I made this year. At least not when it came to you. Howie, relax. You're letting the little things get to you. What's that saying….*Don't sweat the small stuff?* Look," Bryan continued, "As I said before, it's Christmas. You're at a party. Go enjoy yourself, already! Now, if you'll excuse me, my drink's

getting warm. I'm going to go break off part of
Rudolph's antler and cool it down."

Chapter 7

Molly was talking with two of her girlfriends on the other side of the party when Van approached her again. He methodically stepped between Molly and her companions, cutting one of them off in mid-sentence.

"Sorry for that distraction before," Van said to Molly, his back to the other two. "You know what they say…good help is so hard to find." Molly's friends shook their head at Van's unwelcome approach, giggled, and walked away. One gave her a *You're on your own* wave as they left. The other made the *L sign* with her thumb and index finger, mouthed the word *Loser,* and pointed to Van.

"Oh, don't worry about it," Molly said, trying not to laugh at her friends' gestures. "Chuck seemed like a nice guy."

"I suppose. Where's Howard? I get the feeling he's not having a good time tonight."

"He's around here somewhere. And he's fine. He just has a lot on his mind these days."

"If you were my date, I wouldn't leave you alone for a second looking as good as you do tonight," Van said, as he gently grabbed her hand.

Molly's smile disappeared as she immediately jerked her hand back. "Well I'm not your date, so you don't have to worry about it." She was fairly confident that Van's flirting was harmless, but it was his arrogance that offended her even more. That he felt he could touch her whenever he wanted. Like she was an object to possess.

Van continued talking, seemingly oblivious to Molly's sudden change in attitude. "You know this isn't the only Christmas party I'm having this year, right? I still throw my annual Christmas brunch. I invite you to it every year, but you haven't come since you got married."

"I know. We go to church on Christmas morning now. Howard wanted it to be a family tradition for us."

"But what about your friends you miss seeing because of your *tradition*?" Van asked.

"We have friends at church, Van."

Van exhaled heavily, as if he had just succumbed to the fact that he knew he couldn't win the argument. "Alright. All I'm saying is that I miss seeing you at the brunch. So just remember…on Christmas morning, when you're sitting in an uncomfortable pew in a stuffy church sanctuary, you could be here. Enjoying all of…" his voice was suddenly drowned out by the music. Not only had it gotten louder, it wasn't even Christmas music anymore.

Monster Mash by Boris Pickett and the Crypt Kickers was now filling up the great room. Party guests were looking at each other in confusion and laughing amongst themselves. Surely this had to be the first Christmas party in history to feature Halloween songs! A few of the guests even started dancing to it, emulating the

Thriller dance from the famous Michael Jackson video.

Van knew exactly who was to blame. He looked across the room, and his eyes met with Chuck's. Chuck held up both hands, arms fully extended, as if to say *Stay where you are. I've got this.* Van had no intention of staying where he was. "If you'll excuse me," he offered to Molly, with a forced grin. "I have to go kill somebody."

Chapter 8

Van walked with a quicker pace than normal. He nodded and smiled to his guests as he made his way through the crowd to get to Chuck. He even fake-laughed a little at the Halloween song that was still playing in the background. He enjoyed seeing his guests laugh…just not at his expense. That crossed a line. As he approached Chuck, his forced smirk disappeared and his voice lowered. "What do you think you're doing?" he snarled.

Chuck raised his arms above his head as if he were being held at gunpoint. "It's not my fault! All of your holiday playlists are mixed together. You know, you really should separate them by month."

"I think it's pretty clear that *Monster Mash* is *not* a Christmas carol!" Van retorted, his voice raising.

"Look," said Chuck. "We can play the blame game all night long, but where is that going to get us?"

Van stared back in shock and disbelief. "The blame game? But…you…you…you're *obviously* the one to blame!" He was so frustrated, he was actually starting to stutter.

Chuck saw the large vein on the right side of Van's forehead start to protrude and throb.

He put his arm around Van and gently spun him around so that the two of them were now facing the party again. Then he began walking Van back toward the crowd. Van was not used to being touched, much less coerced into moving in a direction against his choosing. He opened up his mouth to protest, but Chuck spoke first. "I can see you're upset. Go mingle with your guests. Relax…I'll take care of this little music mishap. I have some Bing Crosby queued up and ready to go!"

Chuck stopped and Van continued to slowly walk back toward the guests, feeling as if he had just been manipulated. The anger and confusion were mounting at a rapid pace.

"Mr. McNeely!" called Chuck. "Wait a second. I almost forgot something very important." He pulled out another crumpled-up piece of paper from his pocket and headed toward Van. "Each of us on staff tonight is supposed to have you fill out a customer satisfaction survey. You know…based on our performance this evening. Could you take a few minutes and…"

Van's prominent forehead vein now had a secondary vein noticeably branching off from it as his jaw clenched and his hands formed fists by his sides. Chuck surveyed the situation and cautiously took a step backward. "You know what?" he asked as he continued to retreat from Van. "This may not be the best time. I'll just hit you up later. Cool? Cool."

Van stood still, watching Chuck head back to his music duties. Howard's teenage daughter, Heather, passed by and stopped. "Mr. McNeely, are you feeling alright? You look kind of flushed."

Chapter 9

After Van tersely brushed her off, Heather continued through the party crowds until she found her dad. Howard was still standing near the food table, looking as miserable as he had when he first arrived. Heather sidled up next to Howard and put her arm around him.

"Hey, Daddy!"

"Oh, hey, Heather. You enjoying the party?" asked Howard.

"Most definitely," Heather replied sarcastically. "Crappy food, phony people and cheesy Christmas music."

"Believe it or not, that's exactly what I said earlier."

Heather laughed. "Really? That's too funny. Don't get me wrong. You know I love Christmas. I just hate Mr. McNeely's parties. They're nice and all, but it's just not worth hearing him talk about how much they cost him."

"You're preaching to the choir, sweetheart," said Howard.

"You know, you'd think with all the money he *says* he spends on these parties, he could pay a little more attention to detail. Did you know that the Rudolph ice sculpture doesn't even have a nose on it?"

"Imagine that," said Howard, not acting that surprised.

"Well, I just wanted to let you know that Kevin called, and he's going to be here in about ten minutes to pick me up for our date," said Heather.

"Kevin?" asked Howard, playing dumb.

Heather stiffened. "Daddy…we talked about this. You and Mom said it was okay for me to come to the party with you for an hour or so and then go out with Kevin."

"Have I met Kevin?" asked Howard.

"Four times now."

"Do I like him?"

"You must," answered Heather. "This is my fifth date with him."

"Are you meeting him in the driveway, or is he coming inside?"

"He's coming inside."

"Okay. He gets points for that."

Despite being aloof about Kevin to Molly and Heather, Howard knew who he was. He was the kid dating his daughter, so he made sure it was his business to know him. He checked with teachers and other parents to find out if he should have any concerns. So far, somewhat to Howard's disappointment, Kevin was clean. It's not that Howard had anything against Kevin himself. He just wasn't ready for

Heather to be dating. Yes, she was sixteen, but she was also gorgeous. She had long black hair and a slender build. Her big brown eyes, high cheekbones, and flirtatious nature, only added to her allure. Heather was Molly's daughter from a previous marriage that hadn't worked out because her husband, Molly's father, decided he would rather start a new life on his own and not be tied down with a family. Even though Heather was not Howard's biological daughter, it didn't change anything; he loved her as his own.

That was another issue that Howard was struggling with lately. His relationship with Heather. He and Molly had been married for about five years, and Heather had accepted him as openly to the family as Howard had accepted her. Her birth father had left when she was six and only made contact with her on certain holidays. Usually just Christmas and birthdays, although it was not uncommon for him to miss one or two along the way. But now that Heather was a teenager and starting to date, their relationship had become somewhat strained. She was looking for a little more freedom, and Howard was starting to tighten the reigns. It was uncharted territory for both of them, and Howard wondered if either of them was handling the situation the right way.

Over the past year, they had been involved in several severe arguments with Molly always taking Howard's side. Heather had said some hurtful things to him, but had always stopped short of, *You can't tell me what to do. You're not my real dad*! Although he thought he'd seen it in her eyes once or twice. *How do you make someone know that the reason you're not giving them everything they ask for is because you know what's best for them and love them too much to see them make mistakes?* Howard figured that if he knew the answer to that million-dollar question, life would get a little simpler for him.

Heather decided to go on the offensive. She put both hands on Howard's shoulder and rested her head on them. She then looked up at her dad with her big puppy-dog eyes. "Do you know why I think I like Kevin so much?" she asked.

"Why?"

"Because he reminds me so much of you!" said Heather.

Howard smiled. "Flattery will get you nowhere."

Heather flashed her infectious smile at Howard. "Oh well. You can't blame a girl for trying!"

Howard wasn't finished with his interrogation. "Where are you guys going?"

"I don't know," said Heather, rolling her eyes. "Maybe a movie and then a late dinner."

"*What* movie and *what* restaurant?"

"I don't *know* and I don't *know*," replied Heather, mocking Howard by using his own tone against him.

Howard didn't flinch. "Well, let's hope that Kevin has better answers to those questions."

"Oh, Daddy! You're not going to grill him again, are you?"

"First of all," started Howard, "A father can never grill his daughter's date too much.

And secondly…yeah, he's getting grilled. It will probably be the highlight of my night." A smile crept over Howard's face as he thought about it.

"Well, that's just sad," said Heather. "We'll come find you as soon as he gets here."

She bounced back into the party, and Howard watched her go. He wondered how she had grown up so fast. He also wondered if every dad felt as big of a jerk as he did in the way that he tried to protect his daughter.

Chapter 10

First having to talk with Van…and now the thought of having to talk with Kevin, helped Howard with his decision to step out onto the room's adjacent deck and get some fresh air. He opened one of the double-plate glass doors leading outside. Howard stepped onto the plastic-wood composite deck. It had a beautiful sheen to it and completely wrapped around the back of the house. He thought about his own deck at home and how small it was in comparison and how warped and in need of replacing some of his redwood railings were.

Not in the budget, by the way, he reminded himself. He set his drink on the oversized railing and gazed out upon the perfectly manicured sloped lawn. It stretched out about an acre before it turned into a beautiful forest that was all still part of Van's estate. The trees had all lost their leaves, but together were beautiful. It reminded Howard of an Ansel Adams print he had once seen and admired. A couple passed by Howard on their way back inside, leaving him alone on the deck. For a mid-December night, the weather was pleasant to Howard. Maybe around fifty to fifty-five degrees. After being cooped up in the party for so long, and Van causing his blood pressure to rise, the coolness of the crisp winter air was refreshing.

Howard was a God-fearing man as well as a person of strong faith and conviction. His prayers were typically not your run-of-the-mill,

Here's what I need now, God, or *Please let this work out for me,* type of prayers, but more of genuine conversations with the Lord. He thought that was the way God liked it. Being genuine, transparent, real. He also didn't feel that prayer should be limited to church or before going to bed each night. He prayed when and where he felt the need.

This was one of those times. Howard was already feeling lost and dejected, and now compared to the other party guests, he could add *inadequate* to his list of emotions. He was starting to feel anger slowly creep in, so he felt the need to try and circumvent and be real with God. Howard grabbed the railing and looked up into the starless night sky, instead of bowing his head. This was not done out of irreverence, but because he always felt closer to God in the outdoors. By looking up, he had the sensation of actually speaking with God face-to-face.

"Well, God, Merry Christmas…or Happy Birthday. I'm never sure which one is more appropriate this time of year." Howard paused, carefully choosing his next words. "I wish…I wish I could be in a more jovial mood tonight, but I just can't." Howard paused again, searching for the words that best described his feelings. He was wrestling with sounding like a whiner to being brutally honest. "I try to be a good guy. I go to church. I read the Bible. I try to live the life I think you want me to live. But what do I have to show for it? Huh? I'm in a dead-end job where I can barely make ends meet. I'm afraid I'm bringing my best friend down the same road with me. I can't give my wife the life she really wants. My daughter thinks I'm overprotective and gets annoyed with me every time I open my mouth. Life just hasn't turned out the way I thought it would. I always believed that if I truly followed you, everything would turn out great. I know there are bumps along the way, but overall, I thought if I really followed you, that things would be terrific. Here's a newsflash for you. I *have* and they're *not*! I just don't know what to do anymore. I'm out of answers."

Howard wasn't able to finish his thoughts. Chuck suddenly burst through the double doors and onto the deck. He was sweating and out of breath. He looked frantic. He looked both ways before he saw Howard and then sprinted toward him. "Wait! Don't jump!" shouted Chuck.

Chapter 11

"Excuse me?" asked Howard.

Chuck approached Howard slowly, as if he didn't want to make any sudden movements to scare him. "Don't do it. Don't jump. You've got too much to live for," said Chuck in a very deliberate monotone voice.

Howard was confused. "I wasn't going to jump," he answered. "Besides," he gestured to the lawn a few feet below, "We're on the ground level."

"Oh. Well…" stammered Chuck. The two then stared at each other over an awkward silence. Chuck squinted and cocked his head to the side, as if he were studying Howard. Instinctually, Howard then did the same to Chuck. The silence became even more awkward.

Slowly, Chuck pulled out another crumpled-up piece of paper from his pocket. He never took his eyes off of Howard. After unfolding the paper and raising it to eye-level to read it, he glanced back and forth between the paper and Howard. "You *are* Howard Mudd, right?" he asked.

"I am," answered Howard. "And you're the guy who almost gave me goose liver earlier, right? Chuck, if I recall."

"Oh, Howard," said Chuck, smiling. "I'm so much more than that. I've got something to tell you that's going to rock your world. Are you sitting down?"

Howard looked at Chuck, annoyed by the ridiculous question. "No."

"Well, you're going to wish you were when you hear this bombshell. Howard, a drum roll, please," prompted Chuck.

"I'm not giving you a drum roll," replied Howard.

"Not a real drum roll," continued Chuck. "Do it with your mouth…like this,

BRBRBRBRBRBRBRBRBR!" Chuck clinched his jaws, pursed his lips, and blew, giving his best drum roll impersonation.

"I know what you meant," said Howard. "And I'm not giving you one."

"Okay, forget it. Here goes. Howard Mudd…brace yourself. I'm your very own…"

At that exact moment, Dean Martin's *Marshmallow World,* playing in the background, started skipping. Chuck looked back at the party inside and saw Van heading to the music station to remedy the situation. "Oh no!" Chuck said. "McNeely's going to string me up for this one!" He looked back at Howard. "How do digital songs skip, anyway?"

Howard shrugged.

"Don't go anywhere!" he yelled at Howard on his way back to the party. "I'll be back! We really need to talk!"

As Chuck dashed through the door heading inside, he literally ran into Heather and Kevin, who were on their way out to see Howard. Chuck bounced off of Kevin like an all-pro running back, spun around completely, and continued toward Van without losing a second. Howard closed his eyes and wished he were anywhere but this party.

Chapter 12

Howard watched and waited as Heather and Kevin approached. Heather was leading him, holding his hand. He was much taller than Heather. Howard knew that they were both in the 11th grade, but the height difference made him appear much older. He didn't like that. Kevin was wearing jeans and a black t-shirt. *Nice of him to dress up*, thought Howard. His hair was dark brown and parted to the side. His bangs hung dangerously close to his eyes. Howard would have preferred he had a crew cut, but would try not to hold this against him.

"There you are," said Heather. "We couldn't find you. I thought you might have snuck out early."

"I wish," said Howard.

"Daddy, you remember Kevin," she said, stepping to the side to reveal her boyfriend.

Kevin stuck out his hand. "Nice to see you again, Howard," he said.

Howard did not extend his own hand. "Mr. Mudd," he said, forcefully.

"Excuse me?" asked Kevin.

"You can call me Mr. Mudd," said Howard.

Kevin shot a nervous glance at Heather and then back at Howard. "Yes, sir. Of course. I'm sorry."

Howard stared at Kevin until he broke eye contact and looked down at his shoes. Heather finally took charge.

"Well," she began, "As fun as this little get-together has been, we've got to go, Daddy." Heather took Kevin by the hand again and started to retreat. Howard placed his arm in front of her, blocking their passage.

"Where are you taking my daughter tonight?" asked Howard, as if Heather hadn't said a word.

"Dinner and a movie, sir."

"More specific," prodded Howard.

"I was thinking about taking her to the new zombie movie that just came out and then to Mike's Pizza for dinner," answered Kevin.

"What's the new zombie movie rated?" asked Howard.

"I believe it's rated R, sir," said Kevin.

"And you see nothing wrong with taking my daughter to a rated-R movie, Kevin?" Howard continued.

"I...uh...didn't...uh," stammered Kevin, looking down at his shoes again.

"Daddy, that's enough!" interjected Heather, releasing Kevin's hand and squaring off with her father.

"And Mike's Pizza?" asked Howard, again as if Heather hadn't even spoken. "You know they have a bar area in there, don't you?"

"Yes sir," said Kevin.

"*Really*? How would you know that, Kevin?" asked Howard.

"Daddy!" cried Heather again.

"I don't know…I just…we were going to be on the restaurant side," pleaded Kevin.

Howard decided to bring this conversation to an end. "See a PG-13 movie. Make sure you stay on the restaurant side of Mike's Pizza. And have her home by 11:00."

"My curfew is 12:00!" demanded Heather.

"Not tonight it's not," said Howard.

"I can't believe you sometimes!" said Heather. She then turned to Kevin and grabbed his hand again. "Come on, Kevin. We're leaving!"

"I'll have her home by 11:00, sir," Kevin called back, as he was being escorted away.

"I said '*Come on,*' Kevin!" Heather repeated, as she shot daggers at Howard with her eyes. He had never seen her beautiful brown eyes look so hateful.

As Heather and Kevin exited the deck, Chuck passed them as he reemerged. He smiled and nodded, as if to apologize for his abrupt encounter earlier. Heather stormed right past him and appeared to be on a mission to get as far away from Howard as possible.

Chuck looked back at Heather and then over at Howard. "Wow! She did *not* look happy! What did you do?"

Chapter 13

"Sorry, Chuck," said Howard, heading for the door. "I'm not in the mood for talking anymore. If you'll excuse me, I believe there are some cheese cubes calling my name. Oh, and if you don't mind some constructive criticism, it looks like you're on pretty thin ice with Van. I'd get back to work if I were you."

"But, Howard...you *are* my work," said Chuck.

Howard stopped with his hand on the brass door handle. "What are you talking about?"

"Okay. This is it," Chuck said, excitedly. Howard Mudd…allow me to make my formal introduction. I am your very own…"

"Howie! There you are! I've been looking all over for you!" yelled Bryan, walking around the back corner of the deck.

"Oh, come on!" shouted Chuck in frustration, arms flung up in the air.

Bryan walked past Chuck to get to Howard. "Come on, Howie. It's our favorite part of the party. Van's getting ready to give his annual speech where he thanks everyone for coming and pats himself on the back for being such a great guy and throwing such a lavish party. Let's go. It's time to heckle him from the back of the room. Honestly…it's the only reason I come to these things."

"Not tonight, Bryan," said Howard.

"Come on, man!" said Bryan. "I've been working on my one-liners all year!"

"The man said, 'Not tonight, Bryan,' " Chuck said, inserting himself into the conversation.

"Who are you?" asked Bryan.

"I'm Chuck."

Bryan looked at Chuck for a moment. "Yeah. I knew I knew you. You're that guy that yacked in the bathroom earlier, aren't you?"

Chuck shook his head and pretended to laugh. "What? No. I think you have me confused with somebody else."

"No," Bryan continued. "It was definitely you. I was next in line for the bathroom, and I distinctly remember…"

Chuck didn't give Bryan a chance to finish. He physically ushered him back to the door as he was still talking. "Time to go, Bryan. You're going to miss Van's speech. Time to put your zingers to good use. I'll send Howard your way in just a few minutes."

Bryan tried to object, but Chuck pushed him inside and closed the door behind him. He turned back to Howard and smiled. "I thought that guy would never leave," he said.

"Funny," returned Howard. "I was thinking the same thing about you."

"Don't worry about me. I'm not going anywhere," said Chuck.

"Then I am. Have a nice evening, Chuck," said Howard, as he started for the door.

"Wait, Howard. We need to talk," said Chuck, now sounding a bit desperate.

"We've already talked," said Howard, opening the door. "Good night."

"Howard," Chuck called out nonchalantly. "I'm your guardian angel."

Chapter 14

Howard closed the door, leaving the two of them alone outside. "You're my *what*?" he asked, not amused.

Chuck put both hands in his pockets and leaned back against the deck railing, a bit dejected. "I was hoping for more of a dramatic introduction, but…whatever. I'm your guardian angel. What do you think about that?"

Howard smiled. "Okay. I get it. Where are the hidden cameras?" He looked around the perimeter of the deck to see if he could spot any. "You're good. Who put you up to this? It's Bryan, right? It has to be Bryan. This is his kind of humor! Okay. What happens next? I follow you inside to everyone laughing at how gullible I am?"

"What? No. This is real. Bryan has nothing to do with this. Well…at least not this part. I'm a real guardian angel. And I'm really here to help you."

"Nice! Not breaking character," Howard continued. I have to admit…I like your dedication to character. But seriously, what's the end game here? How does the joke end?"

"Hey! I like a good joke as much as the next guy. Believe me, there's a lot of humor in Heaven. But this…right here, right now…is not a joke."

"Chuck…buddy! The gig is up. You were excellent in your role. But I'm just not buying it. So let's go back inside and give Bryan and company their laughs and get on with the party." Howard grabbed the handle on the deck door and tried to turn it, but it didn't budge.

"Sorry, Howard. I can't let you leave that easily. We're not done yet," said Chuck.

Howard's patience started to wear thin. "Look. I told you I like a good joke, but I also told you that this one is over. I don't know how you locked the door, but unlock it. Now."

"No."

"What did you just say?"

"I said, '*no,*'" Chuck repeated. "Not until I convince you that I'm your guardian angel and that I'm here to help you. Just tell me what I have to do."

Howard looked through the pane glass windows of the deck door and saw the party guests mingling and enjoying themselves. He then saw Bryan across the room yawning as Van was talking to him. *If Bryan wasn't interested in what was currently happening on the deck, then he obviously wasn't the mastermind of this prank. Maybe this Chuck guy was just crazy!*

"So?" pressed Chuck. "What do you think?"

"I think you're not making any sense. You're either crazy, or I don't know…maybe you've been dipping into Van's liquor supply. And if he finds out, that's your third strike."

"Howard," Chuck said, shaking his head. "I haven't had anything to drink tonight. I'm working…remember? I'm here to help you."

"Help me to do what exactly?" asked Howard.

"To help you realize that you *are* following the plan God has for you and that your life really *is* terrific. That *was* part of your prayer earlier, wasn't it?"

Howard stared at Chuck, unsure of what to say. "Yeah…now do I have your undivided attention?" Chuck asked, a little arrogantly.

"No," answered Howard. "All that proves is that you were eavesdropping earlier and heard me talking."

"Dude, you don't get it, do you?" asked Chuck. "I've been sent here to help you!"

"And I'm supposed to believe that?" asked Howard. "You've been here all night. I just prayed about five minutes ago."

"Come on, man!" cried Chuck. "You don't think God knows what you're going to pray for before you pray for it? I was planted here tonight because you were going to pray that exact prayer."

"Good answer," replied Howard. "But I'm still not buying it. Now, for the last time…Good night, Chuck. Open the door!"

"Wait," Chuck protested. "What do I need to do to prove to you that I'm your guardian angel and that I've been sent here to help you?"

Howard stared at Chuck as he pondered the question. He figured if he just indulged this guy, he may get back to the party quicker. "Okay. You're an angel, right?"

"Correct."

"And you work for God, I'm assuming."

"Correct."

"And you live in Heaven and are familiar with the Bible."

"Correct and correct."

"Okay, then," continued Howard. If you are truly my guardian angel, recite all the books of the Bible...in order."

Chuck laughed. "Are you kidding me?" he asked. "That's the best you can come up with? Talk about throwing me a softball. Ye asked. Ye shall receive." Chuck ceremoniously cleared his throat before beginning. "Genesis. Exodus…"

Chuck then repeated the two books to himself. Then he looked at Howard. Howard looked back, not surprised. "Two books? You only know two books of the Bible?"

"No! I know them!" pleaded Chuck. "I just get nervous when I'm put on the spot like that."

"Take care, Chuck," Howard said, patting him on the back. "Now… the door."

"Hold on. Give me another shot. What if I were to tell you something about yourself that nobody in the world would know? Then would you believe me?"

"If I play along, will you open the door?" asked Howard.

"Deal."

"Okay. Wow me," prompted Howard. "Tell me something about me that nobody else could possibly know."

Chuck studied Howard carefully, then methodically circled him while thinking. "You're a sports fan," he finally said.

"The good news is that you're right. I am a sports fan. The bad news is that everyone who knows me knows that," Howard insisted.

"Wait a minute. I'm just getting warmed up," continued Chuck. "You're a Baltimore Ravens fan, right?"

"Considering that we're in Maryland, that's not too much of a stretch. Have you got anything else?" asked Howard.

"As a matter of fact, yes. Even though you say you're a Baltimore Ravens fan, you secretly pull for the Indianapolis Colts. And you can't tell anyone because we all know that Baltimore Ravens fans hate Indianapolis Colts fans because the Colts snuck out of Baltimore and, in their words, *abandoned the city and its fans.* How is that?"

Howard stared at Chuck in disbelief and then snapped back into the moment. "You're crazy! I'm a Ravens fan through and through."

"You say that, but secretly, you just couldn't give up watching the players on the Baltimore team you grew up with. You didn't want to keep watching, but you did, and now you still pull for them. And you've never told a soul about this, so this obviously proves…without a shadow of a doubt…that I know things about you that no one else does…proving that I'm your very own guardian angel!"

Howard knew this was true but didn't want to give Chuck the satisfaction of being right. He didn't know how he was privy to this information but would figure that out another time. Right now, he just wanted to get away from Chuck.

"We're done here," said Howard. "Now, we had a deal. I'd engage you in this one last charade, and you'd open this door. If you really believe you're an angel, then I suggest you keep your word. I'm pretty sure they frown upon lying in Heaven."

"Wait! Since you're obviously not going to believe what I say, maybe you'll believe what you see," said Chuck.

"What's that supposed to mean?" asked Howard, now thoroughly exhausted by Chuck's routine.

"Your prayer earlier," said Chuck. "You were concerned that your life hadn't turned out like you thought it should have. That was a selfish prayer, my friend."

"What's that supposed to mean?" asked Howard. He was now annoyed not only by Chuck's statement, but by the fact that he was still engaging him.

"It means that our lives are not just about us," continued Chuck. "They're about the other lives we touch as well. You think your life hasn't turned out the way you think it should have. But what about the other people in your life? What about your loved ones? Friends and family? Their lives are better off because you were in them. And I'm going to prove this point to you. You and I are going to walk back into that Christmas party. It will be the same party with the same guests. The only difference is that…wait for it…you were never born!" Chuck then clapped his hands in excitement.

Howard joined Chuck with mock excitement. "And let me guess…no one will be able to see or hear us, either, right?"

"That's right!" said Chuck. "Have you done this before?"

"No!" answered Howard, losing his patronizing smile and now shouting at Chuck. "But I have seen enough TV shows and movies based on this precise nonsense you're peddling. This isn't exactly an original plot, you know. Take care, Chuck. I'd like to say it was nice meeting you, but…you know."

Howard walked back into the party. Chuck smiled and followed him.

Chapter 15

Howard entered the party, and it was just as he expected. Nothing had changed. It was the same elaborate room. The same upper-crust guests were mingling and talking amongst themselves. Burl Ives' *Holly Jolly Christmas* played in the background. And the food table was exactly where he had left it. He decided it was time to do some damage to the mini crab cakes, so he headed in that direction.

As he popped a crab cake into his mouth, Chuck casually strolled up next to him. "Well?"

asked Howard, with a mouthful of crab. "Nothing's changed. Now will you *finally* leave me alone?"

"Try talking to someone," said Chuck.

Howard dropped his head to his chest in exhaustion. "If I go talk to someone, do you promise you'll leave me alone once and for all?" asked Howard.

"If you want me to, yes," replied Chuck.

"It's a deal," said Howard, as he meandered to the middle of the room.

He passed by a few groups of folks engaging in small talk. He smiled at a few folks, but received no response. He tried again with a few other groups of party guests wrapped up in conversation. Still no luck. In fact, one young lady, an attractive blonde, appeared to look right through him. Howard became a little annoyed as he continued to stroll through the party crowd. Finally, he decided to take the plunge. Though it was out of character, he inserted himself into a conversation between what looked like two couples.

"How are you guys doing?" he asked.

The two couples continued their conversation as if Howard hadn't said a word. "Have you guys tried the goose liver yet?" he continued.

There was still no response. Howard was infuriated. He didn't care how snobby this crowd was, nobody should be treated like this. "Hello!" he shouted in the one gentleman's ear. I know you can hear me!" He then ran his hand up and down in front of the gentleman's face.

He didn't even blink. "Hey! I'm talking to you!" Howard tried to grab the man by his shoulder but his hand passed right through his body. It was a cool sensation, as if he had just dipped his hand into a pond. He immediately jerked back. His hand was ice-cold and had a tingling sensation as if it had fallen asleep. It took a moment to return to normal. The man continued to speak as if Howard had never reached through him. Howard spun around on his heels and studied everyone in the room. *What was happening? Was anyone in here real?*

Howard's look of dismay quickly turned into an expression of frustration. Then he spotted Chuck and his big goofy grin. He made a beeline to him and grabbed him by his shirt, pinning him against the food table. "What's going on here, Chuck?" he demanded.

"Calm down," he pleaded. "I told you exactly what was going to happen. You're seeing life as if you'd never been born. You're going to get a chance to see how miserable your family and friends' lives would be without you."

"I just reached right *through* a guy! How did that happen?"

"Remember, Howard. None of this is real. None of these people are real. God is giving you a glimpse of what life *could* have been like for your loved ones had you not been around."

Before Howard had a chance to respond, he heard the faint clinging of silverware on glass. Then the sound became closer and louder. All of the party guests were tapping their forks or spoons against their glasses to call attention to something. Howard soon realized it wasn't a *something*. It was a *someone*.

"Excuse me. Excuse me," came Van's booming voice from across the room. The party guests moved out of his way like he was Moses parting the Red Sea. "Could I have everyone's attention for just a few moments? I wanted to start by thanking all of you for attending this evening. I know…I know…it's extravagant. I go overboard every year to outdo myself. But for good friends like you…it's worth it." Right on cue, all the guests clapped, with a few whistles thrown in for Van.

Van put up his hands in mock protest, although Howard knew this was the only reason he gave these speeches. "Please, please. Save your applause. If you really want to show your appreciation for tonight's festivities, give it up for my one true love, my beautiful wife…Molly McNeely!"

The crowd applauded as Howard felt his knees start to buckle. He held onto Chuck's shoulder to keep from collapsing. This couldn't be happening. There, standing arm-in-arm with Van McNeely, was his wife, Molly. And she was wearing what appeared to be the most expensive dress he had ever seen.

Chapter 16

Howard stood there, paralyzed. Seeing his wife in the arms of another man…and happy. It felt like he had been punched in the stomach and the throat simultaneously. He was starting to sweat profusely, and his vision was starting to blur. He opened his mouth to speak, but no words came out. He remembered that Chuck said none of this was real, but it was hard not to believe what was right before his eyes.

"You okay?" asked Chuck, as he took a bite of sautéed shrimp off of the skewer he was suddenly holding. "I gotta be honest," he continued. "I did *not* see that coming!"

"What's happening here?" asked Howard, as if he were speaking to no one in particular. He was still leaning on Chuck for support.

"Thank you all so much for coming out tonight," said Molly, now addressing the crowd. Howard heard the words coming out of her mouth, but his eyes were fixed on Van's hand on her bare lower back. "As Big V said, we've spared no expense this year. The champagne and caviar were both imported. So please…eat and drink until your hearts are content. We want to make sure we get our money's worth!" The party guests laughed, as did Van and Molly. Although, the latter came off a bit insincere to Howard.

"Also," Molly continued. "Consider this your formal invitation to come back and join us on Christmas morning for our famous Christmas brunch. This year, I'm happy to announce that in addition to our award-winning Bloody Marys and Mimosas, we will feature four separate omelet bars, each manned by a five-star chef!" The crowd applauded in appreciation, as Molly smiled back at them.

Howard and Chuck continued to watch from the other side of the room. "Four separate omelet bars? That sounds pretty sweet, right?" asked Chuck.

"I don't believe it," said Howard, completely oblivious to Chuck's remarks. "She married Van McNeely. I think I'm going to be sick." Howard turned to Chuck. "Do you believe what we just heard? This is insane."

"I know, right?" asked Chuck. "Who calls their husband *'Big V'*?"

Van's voice abruptly cut through the air and interrupted them. Molly had started to walk away, but Van had grabbed her by the wrist. "Wait a minute, honey," he said to her. "You're not done yet." Molly looked at Van, confused, as the party guests hung on every word coming out of his mouth. "Does everyone love Molly's dress?" Van asked the crowd.

On cue, the guests predictably cheered in response. Her dress was black and form-fitting. It was backless and extended just above her knees. "It was an early Christmas present from yours truly. It's a one-of-a-kind, custom-made dress created by a designer friend of mine in Paris. I shouldn't even say this out loud, but it cost over ten thousand dollars." Guests gasped and let out "*oohs*" and "*aahs*" as they heard the dollar amount. Howard and Chuck rolled their eyes.

"But the price is not important," Van continued. "The more pressing issue is that it just doesn't look right on you, Molly."

Molly looked at Van, stunned. Howard didn't know why he would say this or where he was going with this monologue, but the look on Molly's face devastated him. Van then pulled out a jewelry box from his jacket and opened it in front of Molly. Her hands immediately flew to her mouth in shock. "The dress just doesn't look right on you without these diamond earrings to go with it." Molly wrapped her arms around Van and gave him the tightest hug she could. The rest of the party cheered louder than ever.

Howard continued to watch, glued to the action. The *punch to the gut* feeling that he experienced before, now felt like it was hitting much lower. As he stood there gawking, Molly passionately kissed her *"Big V."*

Chapter 17

"Do you remember when I said I thought I was going to be sick?" asked Howard, eyes still glued to Molly and Van's lip-lock. "Well, now I'm sure of it. He grabbed the closest chair and slumped down onto it. The music started back up, and the noise level rose as the party resumed. Howard and Chuck watched the happy couple walk back through the crowd, holding hands.

"Well, Van may be a tool, but he's right about one thing," offered Chuck. "Those earrings really *do* complete the ensemble."

Ignoring Chuck's feeble attempt to lighten the mood, Howard looked around again for Molly. "Where did they go? I've got to talk to her."

"You can't talk to her, Howard. She's not real, remember?"

"Okay. Okay. I just need to see her again!" he replied.

"There she is," said Chuck, pointing to her as she and another woman strode to the bathroom.

"Come on, let's go!" cried Howard, already in pursuit. Howard and Chuck raced toward Molly as she entered the bathroom with her friend. Howard figured he could just run directly through the other guests, but instinctively was navigating through the crowd, avoiding contact.

Howard stopped at the bathroom door. "Well, what are you waiting for?" asked Chuck.

"Am I allowed to go in there?" he asked.

"Certainly not," said Chuck. "It's occupied. You have to wait your turn."

"You know what I mean," persisted Howard. "I need to see Molly again. Do I use the doorknob, or do I teleport right through the door?"

"Ah! Gotcha! Remember, nothing is real here. You can just walk right through the door."

"Really?" asked Howard. "Okay. Here goes nothing." He took a quick step forward and slammed his face flat on the wooden door. THUNK! Chuck doubled over in laughter. "Are you kidding me?" he asked, trying to catch his breath. "Nobody falls for that!"

Howard held his nose with both hands, while Chuck continued to laugh. "Is this some kind of joke to you?" he asked in a nasally voice.

Chuck quickly composed himself. "No, it's not. I'm sorry. That was unprofessional of me. I just didn't think you would actually fall for it," he said, starting to laugh uncontrollably again. "It's the people who aren't real, not the setting."

Still holding his nose, Chuck raised his head and looked at Chuck. "Is my nose bleeding?"

Chuck drew uncomfortably close and peered up Howard's nostrils. "I don't think so. But you could stand to trim your nose hairs."

Howard shook his head. "I'm going in." He swung open the door and saw Molly and her friend applying lipstick in front of the vanity mirror. He and Chuck quietly walked to the far wall behind them and listened.

"Did you see Nikki's dress?" asked Molly. "Could it have been any tackier? I really should have the invitations read, '*If you're going to buy your dress at Walmart, this party probably isn't for you.*'" Then she and the other woman laughed.

"And what about Vanessa?" asked Molly's friend.

"I know, right?" chimed in Molly.

"Could her facelift be any more obvious? If that were me, I'd be asking for my money back!"

"Rowrrr!" said Chuck in a high-pitched voice, reaching one hand out like he was scratching the air.

"Rowrrr? What's that supposed to be?" asked Howard.

"Rowrr," Chuck repeated. "Like a cat. As in, they're being very catty."

"I know. I've never known Molly to say an unkind word about anyone. Believe it or not, this is harder to watch than her kissing Van."

Molly and her friend continued to talk. "So, do you love the new earrings?" Molly's friend inquired.

Molly shrugged. "Eh. Honestly, I thought they'd be a little bigger. Oh well. They're still nice."

"You're so bad," her friend said, laughing.

"I may be bad, but I'm also worth every penny Big V spends on me!" She put her lipstick back in her purse and checked her hair one last time. Alright, I guess it's time to go back to mingle with the common folks."

"Stop it," said her friend, laughing again. "If it weren't for them, who would we have to make fun of?" This time, they both laughed and walked out of the bathroom.

"What's with her? She's never acted like that before," said Howard.

"Maybe you were never around to keep her grounded," suggested Chuck.

"Let's go. I want to see where she goes next," said Howard.

"She's gone," said Chuck.

"Gone where?" asked Howard.

"*Gone* gone," answered Chuck. "Remember, this Molly…she's not real. This is a *what-if* scenario. As in *what-if* you were never born."

Howard leaned forward. "I thought you were going to show me how miserable my family's life would be without me, had I never been born," he said, through clenched teeth. "This Molly may have a little bit of an attitude, but she looks pretty happy to me."

"Yeah," agreed Chuck. "That was strange. I didn't think it was going to play out like that. Honestly, I don't know what happened."

" 'I don't know'?" asked Howard. "That's your answer? I gotta tell you, Chuck...you're one heck of a guardian angel."

"Really?" asked Chuck, smiling. "Because I have a customer satisfaction survey I need you to..."

"Is there sarcasm in Heaven?" asked Howard, cutting him off.

"Of course there is. Why? Oh, I get it. You don't really think I'm doing a good job. I get it. I'm a bit *hurt*. But I get it."

Howard pushed open the bathroom door, but instead of walking into Van's hallway, he and Chuck were now in what appeared to be an upscale department store. "What's going on now?" asked Howard, as he moved out of the way of busy shoppers passing by. He assumed none of them were real and that they would just walk right through him, but stepping aside was habit.

"You're a tough nut to crack," said Chuck. "So I thought I'd give you one more glimpse into Molly's life without you. Oh…there she is."

Howard saw Molly and a different friend in line to check out. She was wearing a black pant suit with a pink blouse and black pumps. Howard didn't know much about women's fashion, but he knew Molly looked stunning and sophisticated. And he knew the outfit cost more than he probably made in a week. He and Chuck made their way through the crowd to Molly.

"…so I couldn't decide between the Alfani or the Jones New York, so I just grabbed two of each," Molly said to her friend.

"And if it turns out you don't like one, you can always return it," her friend answered.

Molly laughed. "Honey, I don't do returns. I like taking clothes out of stores, not giving clothes back! You should see the back of my closet. If my discard pile gets any bigger, you may not be able to call it a *walk-in* closet anymore."

Both women laughed as they stood in line. An elderly lady was paying for her clothes in front of them by writing a check. "Really?"

said Molly, loud enough for the woman to hear. "Who actually *writes* checks these days? I swear…stores should only accept plastic!"

The elderly lady looked back at Molly and smiled. Molly returned a mockingly insincere smile. "I'll assume since you're writing a check that you have a horse and buggy parked outside, too," she said to the lady.

"I don't understand," said the elderly lady.

"Why am I even talking to you?" Molly asked to no one in particular. "You know what?" she asked, now addressing the salesclerk. "I don't have time for this. You people just blew a big sale. I hope Grandma's fifteen-minute sales transaction was worth it!" She threw all of her outfits onto the counter for someone else to put away and then stormed out of the store. Her friend followed.

Howard didn't say a word, but took off after Molly. Chuck followed them all outside. On the corner of the surrounding sidewalk, a bake sale was taking place. Several youth were either sitting behind a plastic card table with a money box or holding multi-colored poster boards, reading *"Grace Community Church Bake Sale."*

Molly looked at the table and shook her head in disgust. "There should really be some kind of law against this," she said to her friend. "The last thing people want to deal with when they go out is other people begging for handouts! It's appalling!" Howard watched the entire scene unfold as Molly and her friend got into Molly's Bentley and peeled out of the parking lot.

"Pretty ugly scene, huh?" asked Chuck, as he took a bite of a brownie from the bake sale table.

"Where did you get that brownie?" asked Howard.

"The bake sale," said Chuck, pointing behind them.

"Did you get me one?" asked Howard.

"They're not real," replied Chuck.

"But you're eating one," continued Howard.

"It's okay because I'm not really hungry."

Howard stared at Chuck, not knowing how to begin to respond. "So what do you think about Molly now?" asked Chuck, as he shoved the rest of the brownie into his mouth.

"I can't say I approve of the attitude, but I don't mind seeing her have the life she deserves," said Howard.

"What?" cried Chuck through a mouthful of food.

"Molly's the best woman I've ever met and she deserves to be treated like that. Pampered. Spoiled. I just *wish* I could do that for her! Are you telling me that had I never come into her life, she'd be living this way?"

"Wow! The stereotype is really true with people in this life! More often than not, you choose to focus on the wrong things."

"Meaning what?" asked Howard.

"Meaning this night may take longer than I expected. Come on."

Howard followed Chuck back into the department store, but as they walked through the automatic door, the store was gone and they were back at Van's party. "So, is this real life again? Or another *I've never been born* scenario?" asked Howard.

"I'll let you know when we're back to the real world. You have a little more eye-opening to do. We're done with Molly for the time being. Now it's time to check in on a buddy of yours."

As Chuck was speaking, Howard spotted Bryan across the room. "I assume you're talking about Bryan. Let's go see how his life turned out. I just hope it's not as horrible as Molly's.

"But Molly…" began Chuck, before catching himself. "I get it. Sarcasm again, right?"

Chapter 18

Howard and Chuck made their way across the room and approached Bryan. Howard hardly recognized him. Instead of his normal Hawaiian shirt and Santa hat attire, he was dressed in a charcoal Brooks Brothers 1818 suit. With the exceptions of weddings and funerals, Howard had never seen Bryan dressed up, and never in a high-end suit like this one.

Bryan was engaged in a conversation with a well-built, ruggedly handsome man, unrecognizable to Howard. He also wore a designer suit. The closer they got, the more conversation they could hear.

"...so I said if I wanted excuses, I'd ask for them," Bryan said. "What I *do* want is the final product by the end of the month. If that's not an option, I'll find another supplier that can handle the workload."

"So what did he say?" asked the other gentleman.

"He said, 'You'll have it by the end of the month...sir,' " said Bryan. Then they both laughed as if he had just told the punch line to a joke.

"What is he talking about?" asked Howard. "Bryan works on the assembly line at the plant with me. Nobody reports to him."

"That's why you're the youngest plant supervisor the company's ever had. Nobody works harder than you to get results," said the gentleman.

"Yeah, I've definitely paid my dues," said Bryan. "There were a lot of sacrifices along the way, but when it was all said and done…it was worth it. You simply have to prioritize what's important in your life. Then, friend, you reap what you sow."

Bryan and his companion smiled, toasted their glasses together, gulped down some Cabernet, and disappeared back into the crowd. All Howard could think to himself at the moment was that he missed Bryan's Hawaiian shirt. "I need some air," said Howard. He walked past Chuck and out onto the deck. Only, the deck was now gone, and Howard had walked into what appeared to be some sort of upscale restaurant. As he tried to get his bearings, he heard a lot of laughter and commotion from the bar area. He looked over and saw Bryan, along with four other men whom he recognized as upper management from the plant. They were sitting around a high-top table with half-empty highball glasses in front of them. Howard assumed it was after work, as each of them had their jackets off, sleeves rolled up, and ties loosened. Each one of them was smoking a cigar.

Chuck sidled up beside Howard as he watched Bryan and his friends. He couldn't make out what any of them were saying. Each was talking over the next one to the point of yelling. Howard also noticed that their speech was somewhat slurred. Howard found it somewhat odd that Bryan kept checking his iPhone every few minutes. He was never attached to his phone in the past. After a while,

Bryan stood up. "Excuse me, gentlemen…and I use that term loosely," he said to a roar of laughter from his table. "I have to make a trip to the little boys' room. Order another round on me while I'm gone!" His friends held up their glasses to salute him, as he stumbled his way to the bathroom.

Howard noticed that Bryan had left his iPhone on the table. He approached to get a better look. On the screen, it showed seven missed texts from his wife, Kelli. Some of them were visible on the screen. *"When are you going to be home?" "Dinner is getting cold." "You promised you would take Natalie for ice cream tonight." "STILL WAITING!" "Tried to call, but it goes straight to voicemail." "CALL ME PLEASE!"*

Howard backed away from the table. "Feel free to let me off this ride whenever you'd like," he said to Chuck.

"Why? Are you starting to see things a little more clearly now?"

"No. What I see is you twisting things to try and help me feel better. But it's not working!"

"What are you talking about?" asked Chuck.

"What I'm talking about is that Bryan is more successful at work without me in his life. That means he has a brighter future and that he can provide more for his family. Then, because you think I may feel bad about that…and rightfully so, mind you…you decide to show me a one-time occurrence where Bryan goes out with the guys from work and comes home late? Big deal!"

"You know it's a big deal," Chuck shot back. "Bryan doesn't even drink. And NOTHING is more important to him than spending time with his family. Look, things may be going well for Bryan, but you're focusing on the wrong aspects here."

"Aha! So you admit things are going well for Bryan?" Howard asked.

"Well, sure. But they were for Molly, too."

"And there it is! They're both better off without me! You're unbelievable, you know that?" Howard walked out of the restaurant and was now back at Van's party. He was starting to expect the unexpected, so he took his reentry in stride. Chuck ran after Howard, trying to explain himself. However, Howard held up a hand asking Chuck to be silent for a moment.

Chapter 19

Howard turned to Chuck, collecting his thoughts. "Just so I have this straight, because I was never born, I was never a distraction to Bryan at work, and he became plant manager?"

"Plant *supervisor*, actually," replied Chuck. "I think that is an even higher position."

"Whatever!" shouted Howard. "Tell me, Chuck, how is Bryan's life worse without me in the picture? Huh? How?"

Chuck stared up at one of the room's crystal chandeliers for a moment, then closed his eyes. "I got nothing," he admitted.

"Ahhh…this can't be happening!" yelled Howard, grabbing the sides of his head. "Did I really stop Molly and Bryan from being successful and happy just by being in their lives?"

"They both looked happy when you were in their lives, too," said Chuck.

"And successful?" asked Howard.

"It depends."

"On what?"

"On how you define success," answered Chuck.

Their conversation was cut short again by another familiar voice. "Hey, Mom! Hey, Dad!" called Heather as she floated into the room. Van and Molly had reappeared, and she was moving toward them.

"Wait just a minute!" exclaimed Chuck. "That's Heather!"

"I see her," said Howard.

"So, if you were never born…" said Chuck. "Then how is Heather even alive?"

"Seriously?" asked Howard. "She's my stepdaughter. Molly had her before we were married. Could you be any less prepared to work with me? I swear, you act like this is your first assignment."

Chuck remained silent.

"Chuck," continued Howard, spinning toward him. "Tell me I'm not your first assignment."

"Hey, you know what they say," answered Chuck, with a nervous grin. "You've got to start somewhere, right?"

"I don't believe this," said Howard.

Chapter 20

As much as Howard wanted to continue his conversation with Chuck about work experience, he was more concerned with the fact that he had just heard Heather refer to Van as *"Dad."* He moved over to where this *new* family was gathered.

"I'm heading out for a while. I'll be back later," Heather said. She hugged Molly and then gave Van a peck on the cheek.

"Have fun, sweetheart," Molly said.

"Have fun?" repeated Howard. He was now walking toward Molly and speaking to her as if she could hear him. "Have fun? How about, *Where are you going? Who are you going out with? When will you be home?* Nothing? Just, *Have fun?*"

"Heather, wait," Van interjected.

"Finally," said Howard. He was somewhat relieved that some parental guidance was finally being shown. *Even if it was from Van.* "Thank you!"

Van pulled his wallet from his jacket. "Here's some money for tonight. Go have yourself some fun!" He handed Heather a wad of cash that Howard thought looked like more than one of his paychecks.

"Thanks! You're the best dad ever!" said Heather, as she hugged Van. As Howard watched, he wasn't sure which was more painful…Van replacing him as a husband or Van supplanting him as a father.

Van laughed as the hug ended. "No, you're the best. Go on. Get out of here, and have a good time!" A car horn blared from outside. Two short blasts followed by a long one.

"That's Kevin," said Heather. See you guys!" Heather ran through the crowd toward the door.

"Tell Kevin we said 'hello,' " called Van. "I really like that boy," he said to Molly.

"They let him blow the horn to pick her up? He doesn't have the decency to come inside to get her and they're okay with that?" asked Howard through clinched teeth. He could feel his temper flaring. He instinctively started after Heather. "Heather! Tell Kevin to get his butt in here RIGHT NOW! I want to have a word with him!"

"Howard, they can't…" started Chuck.

"I know they can't hear me!" yelled Howard, now taking his frustration out on Chuck. He walked around in circles for a moment, trying to collect himself. It didn't work.

"I need some air!" said Howard. And he headed back to the deck.

Chapter 21

Chuck closed the deck door behind him as he followed Howard outside. The cool air felt good to Howard, as he knew his blood pressure was up. A few flurries falling wet upon his face would have felt even better, but he'd take what he could get. Howard paced back and forth, staring at his shoes, while Chuck stood still, not really sure of what next step to take.

"So, Chuck," said Howard, being the first one to break the ice. "Since you're obviously new to all of this, allow me to recap this evening for you. And you tell me if I'm off-base at all on anything I'm saying. Okay? You're assigned to me as my guardian angel because I'm having some doubts about how I'm living my life and the choices I've made. Am I right so far?"

"So far, but…"

"And then," Howard continued, cutting off Chuck. "You came up with the bright idea of showing me what life would be like had I never been born. Why this is the game plan you chose, I have no idea. Maybe it's because you're about as original as you are competent."

"Now wait just a minute…"

"And you told me you're showing me this life because all the people closest to me are better off because I'm in their lives. Well, Chuck, am I getting all of this right?"

"Well, technically yes, but…"

"Then I had the distinct pleasure," continued Howard, growing angrier as he spoke. "Of watching my wife being married to the most pompous jerk on the face of God's green earth. And if that's not bad enough, I got to watch him pamper her with the kind of life she wants…the kind of life she deserves…the kind of life that I can't give her! Jump in any time, Chuck. Let me know when I stop being accurate!"

"If you'd just calm down for a moment…"

"But the show wasn't over yet, was it Chuck? I then got to see my best friend as a big shot plant manager…"

"Supervisor," Chuck inserted.

"Excuse me! Supervisor!" Howard corrected. "I got to see my best friend as a big shot plant supervisor with all the money and prestige that go along with it! And why is he the plant supervisor? It's obvious, isn't it? I was never born to be a distraction to his career! I'm a heck of a guy, aren't I, Chuck?"

"Look, I don't think it's as simple as…"

"And then…the icing on the cake! You entered my daughter into the scenario. She's loving life. No questions asked by her parents. No…they trust her! They give her money! You know what? I've never seen her happier! But do you know what the final straw was, Chuck? Do you? I got the distinct pleasure of standing three feet away from my daughter and watch her tell Van that he's the, *'Best Dad Ever!'* *Van McNeely… 'Best Dad Ever!'* " Howard held his hands up in dramatic fashion as he said the words *Best Dad Ever*, as if he were placing them on a marquee sign overhead. He then theatrically brought his arms back to his chest as if to stab himself with an imaginary dagger to the heart, which he continued to thrust three times for effect. "Do you know how many times Heather has told me that *I'm* the best dad ever?"

"One hundred?" Chuck feebly guessed.

"Zero!" screamed Howard. "Never! Not once has she ever referred to me as the best dad ever. She's usually telling me to chill out or calm down!"

"Imagine that."

"I try to be a good dad, but I'm obviously making my daughter's life miserable. So after all that, what's the lesson to be learned here tonight? I'll tell you. My wife...my daughter…and my best friend's lives *suck* because I'm in them! Bang up job, angel! I guess your work here's done. I feel one hundred percent better!"

"Look, Howard, I know you're upset. But I'm sure there's a perfectly good explanation for all of this."

"There is?" asked Howard, sarcastically. "Fantastic! Don't keep me in suspense. What is it?"

"I have no idea."

Chapter 22

Chuck's incompetence was coming as less and less of a surprise to Howard as the night progressed. "You have no idea," Howard repeated, letting the words sink in. "Of course. Why, after all that we've been through tonight, would I think you would have any idea? How silly of me!"

"Wait," said Chuck. "I said *I* have no idea. But I know there's a perfectly good explanation. And I'm going to find out what it is."

"How?" asked Howard.

"Have you forgotten whom I work for?" asked Chuck. "Just let me touch base with headquarters and find out what's going on here. It's all going to be fine. In fact, I bet we'll be laughing about this sooner than you think."

Howard shook his head in disagreement as he watched Chuck pull out a phone from inside his cummerbund. But it was not just any phone. It looked like an original flip phone from the '80s. It was metallic gray and almost as thick as it was long. It had oversized number buttons on the face and a few additional ones on the side. Howard wondered how Chuck had even concealed it behind his shirt.

"That's how you touch base with Heaven?" asked Howard.

"Yeah, pretty cool, huh?" returned Chuck, as he extended a long silver antenna from the top of the phone.

"Are you telling me that Heaven doesn't have some advanced technology? Something better than we have on Earth? Why aren't you at least using Bluetooth?" Howard continued.

"Heaven's technology blows away Earth's technology. And yes…we have Bluetooth. But have you seen those things? I'd look like an idiot with that thing on my face." Chuck then lifted his clunky phone to his ear and began to talk as Howard shook his head at the irony.

"Yes, this is Chuck. Clearance code: 41872. I need to speak with whomever is on duty regarding the Howard Mudd case. Yes, I'll hold." Chuck was not surprised to hear that Chuck didn't even have the clout to get through to someone immediately. He felt that being placed on hold said a lot about Chuck's place in the pecking order of Heaven. And the fact that he was assigned to Howard as his guardian angel spoke volumes about where he stood with God. Every single thing about this night was starting to annoy Howard more and more. Like the fact that Chuck was even using a phone in the first place.

"Can't you just disappear and then reappear in Heaven, and talk with someone face-to-face?" asked Howard.

"Now who's been watching too many TV shows and movies?" asked Chuck.

"So it doesn't work that way?" asked Howard.

"No, it totally does," Chuck said smiling. "I was just kidding. But rule number one, Howard, is, *'Never leave your wingman.'* "

Howard stared back at Chuck. "That's you, Howard," he said.

"I get it," said Howard.

Chuck diverted his attention back to the phone. "Yes, I'm here. Go ahead." He then held up a finger to Howard, letting him know that he would just be a minute, and walked to the back corner of the deck for some privacy.

Chapter 23

Howard was by himself again. Earlier in the evening, he had enjoyed being alone. Now, the solitude was somewhat depressing. He longed to be with Molly or Heather or even Bryan again. *The real versions*, not the fabrications he had just witnessed. But then he wondered if that was even fair to them. Were they truly better off without him? Or had Chuck just messed that up royally? From what he knew of Chuck so far, he thought there was a fighting chance that could be the case. But what if it wasn't?

He looked up at the night sky again. A few shining stars were now poking out from the dark purple backdrop high above him. One star shot across the night, and he wondered if there was any significance to that. He realized he was standing in the exact same spot he had been earlier when he prayed. Had God actually heard his previous prayer and answered by sending Chuck? *I didn't think God made mistakes*, he thought. Or had his prayer simply fallen on deaf ears like he felt so many of his had lately.

"Well, here we are again, God," began Howard, looking up to the stars. Howard didn't know if he even felt like praying again. But he didn't know what options he had, either. "For the first time in my life, I honestly don't know what to say to you. I came to you earlier because I was having questions about the way that I was living my life. I feel like I've been faithful to you, but what do I have to show for it? Not much. Then you, in your infinite wisdom, validate that my life is not only meaningless, but actually detrimental to the ones I love the most. I just don't get it. How about…how about Galatians 6:9? *'And let us not get tired of doing what is right, for after a while we will reap a harvest of blessing if we don't get discouraged and give up.'* I guess that's just some bone you throw at us to keep us in line, huh? Well, I have to tell you, after what I've seen tonight…I'm done. I'm done with church. I'm done with the Bible. And I'm especially done with you."

Howard knew it was a bold statement that he had just made, but it was how he felt. A small part of him wondered if he should brace himself to be struck by lightning. But that didn't happen. In fact, nothing happened. Just as he'd come to expect, God remained silent.

Chapter 24

"You're going to love me!" shouted Chuck, reappearing from around the back corner of the deck.

"Be careful what you wish for, Chuck," answered Howard. "You've seen what happens to the people I care about."

"I figured out what the problem is," Chuck continued, ignoring Howard's shabby attempt at humor. "Well, *I* didn't figure it out, but I do know why things happened the way they did."

"Why?"

"Because I showed you the wrong time points," explained Chuck.

"Like I'm supposed to know what that means," said Howard.

"Time points…they're just like they sound. Points in time. The ones I showed you were too far back. We need to see time points for Molly, Bryan, and Heather that happen much later in their lives."

"I still don't get it," admitted Howard.

"We only saw a small glimpse of their lives without you. We need to go further into their future to get the full picture. Let's go." Chuck started toward the door leading back into the party.

Howard didn't budge. "Hold on, Chuck. I'm telling you right now. I can't take any more surprises like last time. Tell me you know what you're doing."

"Trust me," said Chuck. His playful demeanor was now gone. His voice, more somber. "You're going to want to see this."

Chapter 25

Howard followed Chuck back into the mansion. However, this time there was no party. There were no decorations. There were no guests. No music, no food, nothing. In fact, they weren't even in the great room. They were in what appeared to be Van's office. Howard had been in this room once before, years ago, when he got lost at one of Van's parties trying to find the bathroom.

Mahogany bookshelves lined the exterior walls of the room, filled with perfectly straightened hardback books, ranging in all sorts of business topics from law to real estate investing. Several diplomas and various awards were matted, framed, and displayed on the wall behind Van's desk that matched the bookshelves.

The blinds were drawn on the floor-to-ceiling windows on the farthest wall, so that the only light in the entire room came from a desk lamp. It took Howard's eyes a few moments to adjust to the darkness, and that's when he saw Van behind the desk. He wasn't wearing his jacket anymore. In fact, he had on a button-down shirt with the sleeves rolled up to his elbows. Howard had never seen that look on Van before. He actually looked like he was working hard! He was poring over some typewritten papers strewn all over his desk, and Howard noticed beads of perspiration on his forehead. Then he saw Molly emerge from the darkness behind Van and put her hands on his shoulders. She wore an expression on her face that Howard had never seen before and instantly knew he never wanted to see again. She looked dejected, beaten, heartbroken.

"I don't understand, V," said Molly. "How did this happen?"

"I don't know," answered Van. He never looked up from his papers. "I just don't know. My accountant assured me this investment couldn't miss. He said to go all in with 2nd *Story Communications*. It was a sure thing."

Howard saw a look in Molly's eyes that showed him that she wanted to speak, but was scared. "But, it's true? It's all gone? Everything?"

Van couldn't look at her. He showed all the signs of a beaten man, a look that Howard had never seen or thought he ever would, on Van. "I'm afraid so. I sank everything we had into this. We've got nothing left."

Molly started to weep. "What are we going to do, V? We lost everything! We lost everything!" Her sobbing became more uncontrollable as Van sat quietly, not doing anything to console her.

Howard had seen enough. He turned around, headed straight out of the office door, and found himself back on the deck where they had started. Chuck followed closely behind him. That *punch-to-the gut* feeling had returned for Howard.

"Sorry, Chuck. I don't know if we were finished in there or not, but I just couldn't be in there for one more second watching Molly cry like that."

"It's okay. You saw enough."

"You know what?" Howard blurted out, trying his best to rationalize the situation. "Big deal. So they lost money. Van's a smart guy. He can rebuild. They'll land on their feet. There's really not that much to get upset over. Right?"

"That's not what this is about. I'm afraid you're not seeing the big picture. Maybe another trip inside will help clear things up for you."

"Do I have a choice?" asked Howard. He didn't even wait for a response. He walked back into the mansion.

Chapter 26

As they reentered, Howard noticed that not only were they not at Van's party, they weren't even in Van's mansion now. A musty smell overtook him as he surveyed the surroundings. There was not much to take in. They seemed to now be in some kind of studio apartment. The kitchenette, single bed, futon, and card table and chair were all within twenty feet of one another. A few empty pizza boxes and beer cans were on the shag carpet next to an overflowing trashcan holding more of the same.

There were no pictures on the walls giving it any kind of a homey, lived-in feel at all.

Howard was startled when someone else walked through the door behind him. It was Bryan. He was dressed in a t-shirt and jeans, a far cry from the last outfit Howard had seen him in. He was talking on his cell phone, and his usual smile was gone.

"I love you, too, Natalie. I can't wait to see you in a few weeks," he said, then shut his eyes tightly, as if the last words were painful leaving his mouth. "Can I speak to Mommy, now? Hey, Kelli…No, the alimony check is going to be a little late this week…I'll get it to you, though. I promise…We just got word that the plant's being sold….No. Everyone's job is safe except for management…I know. I've already looked for jobs around here, but nobody's hiring….Yeah, I have a pretty solid lead on one, but it's about two hours away. I'd have to move…I know, but I don't think I could stand to be that far away from Natalie…or you…No, I know. I'll do what I have to do to make things right. I love…"

Howard heard a click and knew that the phone had been hung up on the other end. Bryan absently tossed his phone onto the futon and grabbed a can of beer out of the refrigerator. He sat down at the card table which doubled as his kitchen table and leaned forward, resting his head on his hands, between his knees.

Howard stood next to Bryan's still frame, hunched over and beaten. "You have to be kidding," said Howard, kneeling down to look face-to-face at an oblivious Bryan. "Bryan and Kelli are divorced? They had a great marriage. How did this happen? And now he lost his job? I don't get it."

Chuck gently put his hand on Howard's shoulder. "Let's go."

Howard stole one last glance at Bryan before leaving through the door in which they entered. Like last time, neither Chuck nor Howard spoke for a few moments. Howard was digesting what he had just seen, and Chuck was giving him time to do just that.

"And to think," Howard finally said. "Earlier in the night, my definition of *depressing* was Van's party. But this…I don't think I can take any more."

"We're almost done," prompted Howard. "Only one more trip."

Howard's eyes squinted as he figured out what Chuck meant. "Not Heather. I'm warning you right now. I refuse to watch anything bad happen to my child."

Chuck didn't speak, though his eyes told Howard he felt his pain. "Okay. Let's go ahead and get this over with. It's not like I have a choice, do I?" asked Howard. He walked past Chuck and back through the door.

"I never said this was going to be fun," Chuck muttered to himself.

Chapter 27

Something new happened when Howard crossed the threshold from the deck to inside this time. It actually became colder. He could see his breath in front of his face. There was a definite breeze blowing at him. He looked back at the door that he and Chuck had just walked through, and it was now an industrial-sized metal door against a worn brick façade on the side of a five-story building.

He was standing on a snowy sidewalk, just off of an alley, next to a bus depot. Faintly at first, but becoming more prominent, were the sounds of the city: horns blaring from passing cars, chatter from people passing by on the sidewalks, the roar of engines ranging from motorcycles to commercial trucks. Then there were the ever-present police sirens. Howard spun around, trying to get his bearings.

"Where are we?" he asked.

Chuck didn't answer, but nodded his head in the direction of the bus depot sign. Howard looked that way, but didn't see anything. Then, as a crowd of people scurried past, he saw her. Heather. Sitting on the bench underneath a streetlight, looking scared for her life.

"Heather!" Howard instinctively yelled. "Heather! Over here!"

Heather was unfazed by Howard's shouts. In desperation, he turned back to Chuck. "What is she doing in the city all alone?"

"She's not alone, Howard."

Howard directed his attention back to his daughter. That's when he saw a young man worming his way in-between shuffling pedestrians, slithering through the crowd to join her. *Kevin!*

Kevin sat down next to Heather and put his arm around her. He rubbed her back up and down, as if he were trying to warm her up. They smiled at each other, but Howard knew that Heather's was forced.

"I told you everything was going to be alright, didn't I?" Kevin asked. "Remember, if we can make it here, we can make it anywhere!" He then forced a laugh.

Howard turned back to Chuck. "They're…we're…in New York?"

"I can't wait to start our new life together," Kevin continued, then leaned in and kissed her. "We'll meet up with my cousin in an hour. He said we could crash at his apartment with him and his roommates until we find a place of our own. We'll get a good night's sleep tonight and then hit the streets tomorrow, looking for work."

"Work? What about school? Besides, what kind of jobs are they even qualified for?" asked Howard.

As if to answer him, Kevin continued. "My cousin knows a guy who knows a guy who's going to hook you up with a fake ID. He's the same guy who got me mine. Once we have those, it will be no problem for us to find jobs bartending or waiting tables. This is going to be awesome!"

"If you say so," said Heather, unconvincingly. "You know I trust you."

Kevin leaned in and gave Heather a longer, more passionate kiss. Howard's eyes widened. "Chuck, I know they can't see us or hear us, but please tell me they can feel us, because I'm about to tear Kevin apart limb by limb!"

"And that's our cue to leave," said Chuck, grabbing Howard and spinning him in the opposite direction, back toward the door.

"No. Not yet. I can't just leave my daughter…or my fake daughter…whatever she is…like this. What happens next, Chuck?"

"Come on." Chuck led Howard through the rusted metal door in the brick building behind them. It was pitch dark, and Howard had a hard time adjusting his eyes to the blackness. He coughed at the overwhelming smoke they were now engulfed in. As they continued down a damp corridor with his shoes sticking to the floor with every step he took, he eventually made out a light in the distance ahead. Then the smoky smell started to give way to a stale beer smell. Howard preferred the smoke. As they stepped into an open room, Howard saw that they were in a dive bar, somewhere in the city, he assumed.

The lighting was dim in the small room. A bar that sat about ten customers wrapped around the wall next to another eight tables. The only entertainment seemed to come from a TV hanging over the bar, an old dartboard with a few numbers missing, and a jukebox that didn't look like it had been serviced since the '80s. ACDC's, *Highway to Hell* was blaring from it. Jeans, t-shirts, and leather vests or jackets seemed to be the attire of choice in here. There were a few patrons who had apparently been *over-served* and were sleeping it off at the bar.

Howard had an idea as to why they were here, but was hoping to God that he was wrong. Then he saw her and knew that he wasn't. Heather walked into the room as if from nowhere. She was wearing a skirt so short that it didn't even come close to ending at her knees. A tight t-shirt donning a cartoon rodent with the name *RAT TRAP* written across the chest, was tucked into the skirt she was wearing. Howard assumed that was the name of the hellhole they were frequenting. It was also not lost on him that Heather was wearing more makeup than he had ever seen her apply. She carried a tray full of four mugs of beer to a table in the corner.

"Here you go, gentlemen. Enjoy," said Heather as she placed the drinks on the table. The four men in sleeveless t-shirts didn't say a word at first as they took their beers. Then, as Heather turned to leave, one shouted, "And keep 'em coming," as he slapped Heather on her backside.

Heather turned around and smiled in faux shock. "You boys better behave yourselves," she called back, as she continued to the bar. As she walked away, Howard saw her expression lose its smile and turn to a look of desperation. No one else would have noticed but a daddy, but Howard knew his little girl was close to tears.

———————

177

Howard knew the rules. He had been at this for a few hours now. He knew nothing in this scene was real, and none of its players were real. But that didn't matter to him at this point. He walked over to the table Heather had just served and calmly said, "Get up. All of you."

The four continued to drink their beers in silence. "I said, *'Get up,'*" Howard repeated. When nothing happened for a second time, Howard took matters into his own hands. He tried to grab the man who had dared touch his daughter, but both arms drifted right through the man's shoulders. Out of frustration, Howard pulled back and then took a swing at the man sitting to the right of the culprit. His fist swung forcefully through the patron's jaw. Howard swung one more time, with the same results.

Howard then backed up and stared at the table. With a wild look in his eyes, he pleaded with Chuck. "Just for five minutes. That's all I need. Just five minutes. Make them real, Chuck. Give me a shot at them. You can't tell me they don't deserve what's coming to them."

"I can't," stated Chuck. I can't tell you they don't deserve to be taught some manners. But I also can't make them real for you. Let's go."

Howard was breathing heavily, and his forehead had become sweaty. He stared at the men one last time. Then he looked for Heather. He found her at the bar flirting with an older man drinking a gin and tonic. He knew the flirting was fake, but also knew that this was her life now. It was all he could do to fight back the tears.

Chapter 28

"What's gotten into her?" asked Howard, once they were back in the real world. He was pacing frantically back and forth again. His sadness now turned to anger and frustration. "She has better sense than that!"

"Speaking of sense, is any of this making *sense* to you yet? Are you starting to connect the dots?" asked Chuck.

"What do you mean?"

"I mean, now that you've seen life in the long run for your family and friends, are you starting to understand the message being delivered to you tonight?" asked Chuck.

"Not really," answered Howard. "What? Because I was never in their lives, they became poor or unemployed or ran away? Again, in the whole scheme of things, big deal! Van will make more money, and Molly will get the pampered life she deserves. Bryan…he's got a lot going for him. He'll find another well-paying job and find a way to work things out with Kelli. And Heather…well, she's a bright girl. She'll come to her senses, dump that loser, Kevin, and return home. They'll all be fine and will *still* be better off without me."

"You still don't get it, do you?" asked Chuck. "Yeah, they may all be fine because they work themselves out of the situations we just saw. But then the cycle will continue. It will happen again and again and again. And do you know why? It's because of what they choose to invest in."

"Quit speaking in riddles, man! It's late. I'm frustrated. Just tell me what you're trying to say."

"What I'm saying is that it all comes down to investments."

"Yeah," agreed Howard. "I saw what happened to Van and Molly."

"Not investing with money," corrected Chuck. "Investing with your life."

"Okay..." Howard prompted.

"Take Van and Molly, for instance," continued Chuck. "Look what fueled their lives. Money. It was their identity. It was their purpose. It was their livelihood. It was what made them who they were. And they chose that path. Everything they did, every sacrifice they made, was for money. They put all their eggs in one basket, and look what happened."

"They lost it all," answered Howard.

"They lost it all," repeated Chuck. "Because money can be easily lost. Now what about Bryan?"

"What *about* Bryan?" Howard shot back.

"Look what he invested in."

"He invested in his work…his career. That's *not* a bad thing," said Howard.

"No. It's not a bad thing," agreed Chuck. "As long as it doesn't come at the expense of more important things in life. As long as it doesn't define who you are as a person."

"And that's what happened to Bryan?" asked Howard, almost defiantly.

"Bryan decided that getting ahead at work was more important than time with family and time at church."

"We all have to make sacrifices now and then. That's just life!" justified Howard.

"Hey, I get that," said Chuck. "But it's a slippery slope. Once you give work more and more of your time, it gets easier and easier to give your family less and less." He paused for a moment to let Howard process what he had just said. "And then, there's Heather."

"Wait a minute, Chuck," interrupted Howard. "I think I may be catching on here. Heather's bad investment…relationships with losers?"

Chuck let out a laugh before he could stop himself. "Yeah, but why don't we just go with *relationships*? Sure, Heather may wise up and leave Kevin, but the pattern will repeat itself. Just like it will for Van and Molly and for Bryan. And it all boils down to poor investments."

"Okay. I get your point, but I still don't see how their lives were better off with me in them," admitted Howard.

"You still don't see it, Howard? You were their personal investor."

Chapter 29

"Right..." said Howard, skeptically, drawing out the one-syllable word. He was afraid that he was starting to fall behind in the conversation again. "I think we're on the same page here, but go ahead and tell me what you mean, just to confirm."

"With pleasure. You see, you personally helped each one of them invest in something a lot more secure than money or power or relationships. In fact, you had them invest in something that they can never lose."

"I'm sorry," said Howard, desperately trying to keep up with Chuck's explanation. "You had me, and then you lost me again."

"Before you started dating Molly, she and Heather never went to church. You introduced them to that, remember?"

"Yeah."

"Well, you've been going to church as a family ever since you married her. Molly's involved in the women's ministry, and Heather is a part of the church youth group. These associations became part of who Molly and Heather are. They invested their lives in these areas because you helped lead them there. The same goes for Bryan. Do you remember why he didn't put in that extra overtime this year?"

"Not specifically."

"Two reasons," continued Chuck. "The first is that you told him you thought that overtime was taking away too much family time from you guys. You led by example and cut back your overtime hours. Bryan watched and followed your example. The second reason is that you started that Bible study last summer. Remember? You don't know this, but Bryan had the opportunity to put in extra hours, but chose not to. Instead, he came and supported you by joining your study. In other words, he chose to invest in family and God's word. Guess who nudged him down that path?"

"Me?"

"It was a rhetorical question, Howard, but yes…you. These folks, the ones that you are closest to, are better off because you were in their lives to help point them to an eternal investment. And because of that, you'll get to spend the next couple hundred zillion years with them. There's no greater privilege than that."

"I…I don't know what to say."

"Oh, I'm not done, dude. I'm on a roll now! The next time you want to feel sorry for yourself about money, remember this. Money may be tight, but it has always been there for you. And when you wonder why you never got ahead at work, think about the plant being sold in the future. You're not management, so your job will be safe. Remember, you're part of a bigger plan and whether it feels like it or not, you're always being watched over and taken care of. And let me fill you in on one last secret. When Heather gets annoyed with you as a father, deep down, she's glad she knows how much you care. So the next time the role of dad feels like a tough one, just remember. There's another Father who's underappreciated and second-guessed all the time. Yet, He remains diligent in His parenting, as well."

As the reality of the situation settled in, Howard's eyes watered up, and his throat started to constrict. He fought back every urge he had to cry. He didn't know why this was happening. Was it out of joy? Revelation? A fuller understanding of God's love and grace for him? The feeling was overwhelming, and he was scared that if he started…if he let the dam burst, he might be bawling with Chuck for a good long while. Instead, he cleared his throat and wiped away the tears from his reddened eyes.

He put his arm out to Chuck to shake hands in the manliest way he could. Chuck looked at Howard's hand, walked right past it,

and gave Howard the tightest hug he'd ever
received.

Chapter 30

Howard finally patted Chuck on the back to let him know it was time to break the hold. Chuck released and backed away. Howard saw that now both of them were teary-eyed. "Thank you, Chuck," he said. "I don't quite know what to say…except *thank you*."

"You don't need to say anything. It's been my pleasure. You stay on the course you've been on, and keep doing what you're doing. There are a lot of other people in the world who could use some good investment advice."

"I'll keep that in mind," said Howard, smiling. "So what happens now? Do we hear a bell, and you get a pair of wings?"

"Again with the TV shows and movies..." said Chuck, returning the smile.

"Well, I think I'm going to head back inside to the party. I'm assuming it's back to being a party?"

"Everything's back to normal," Chuck confirmed.

"Are you coming?"

"No," said Chuck. "This is the end of the line for me. You take care."

"Wait," started Howard. "Will I ever see you again?"

"Maybe. Maybe not. But I'll be watching over you. You know…that whole *wingman* thing."

"Take care, Chuck," said Howard, reaching out and shaking his hand. "And stay away from the goose liver!" Chuck laughed.

"Were you serious about that customer satisfaction survey you mentioned earlier? I'm happy to fill it out," said Howard.

"Oh…about that. I wasn't sure if you were going to have time for that," said Chuck, somewhat embarrassed, pulling the balled-up form from his pocket and showing that it had already been completed. "I took the liberty of filling it out for you. All 10s okay?"

"Absolutely," said Howard. And with that, he left Chuck on the deck and returned to the party.

Chapter 31

As soon as Howard opened the door, the sounds and the warmth of the party overwhelmed him. Boney M.'s, *Mary's Boy Child,* played in the background as the guests mingled and danced. It didn't take long for Howard to spot Molly. He found her and moved in like a man on a mission.

"There's the most beautiful woman at the party," he said as he approached. Then he grabbed her by the hand, twirled her around, and dipped her.

"Okay. Who are you and what have you done with my husband?" asked Molly, laughing. "Oh, never mind. I like you better."

Howard continued to hold Molly lowered in the dipped position. "I just wanted to tell you that I love you. And I love that dress," he said. And then he kissed her, his first public display of affection in as long as Molly could remember.

"And I like whatever it is you're drinking!" said Molly, as she was returned to an upright position.

"Straight tonic water," said Howard.

Their banter was cut short when they saw Heather heading their way. "Sweetheart, what are you doing back already?" asked Molly.

"I don't know. I...I just decided to hang out here with you guys instead. If that's okay," answered Heather.

"Of course. Is everything alright?" prompted Molly.

"Yeah," said Heather. "But I don't think I'm going to be seeing any more of Kevin. It turns out he *did* want to go to the bar side of Mike's Pizza."

"That's crazy," said Molly. "How did he expect to get served?"

"Probably with his fake New York ID," said Howard.

"How did you know about that?" asked Heather.

"I just assumed that if he was going to a bar underage, that he would have a fake ID," explained Howard.

"How did you know it was from New York?" asked Heather.

Howard smiled at Heather and gave her a side hug. "A father just knows these things. I'm glad you're here with us tonight."

Howard then saw Bryan making his way across the room. "Would you ladies excuse me? There's someone else I need to speak with."

Chapter 32

Howard made his way through the party crowd, smiling, laughing, and making small talk with everyone he passed. He finally made his way to his best friend.

"Bryan! What's up, man?"

"Nothing, Howie. What's up with you?" he asked.

"Just having a blast at this party," said Howard.

"Since when?" asked Bryan, somewhat confused.

"Since I had a talk with someone about investments," answered Howard.

"Did I hear someone say something about investments?" came a recognizable voice from behind. Van McNeely appeared and put his arms around both Howard and Bryan. "I just received the hot tip of the century from my accountant. A small business on the verge of a huge breakout. It's called 2*nd* *Story Communications*. According to him, this one *can't miss*. Do you two want in?"

"Van, I can honestly say, with no hesitation whatsoever, that I'm going to pass on this one."

"Me, too," echoed Bryan.

"And I'm no stock expert," continued Howard. "But my gut says you should pass on this one, too, Van."

Van laughed his most arrogant laugh. "You're right. You're not a stock expert, Howard. Let's see, to whom should I listen? My high-priced accountant or your cheese cube-filled gut?" Van laughed again. "Oh well, don't say ol' Van didn't try to help you guys out. I'm going *all in* on this one!"

As he walked away, Howard shook his head, for the first time ever, feeling sorry for Van. He then snapped his attention back to the party at hand. "Do you want to do something fun?" he asked Bryan.

"Like what?"

"Do you want to stuff the rest of the Rudolph ice sculpture into Van's Porsche?"

A mischievous grin crept over Bryan's face. "Just try and stop me!" The two took off in a dead sprint to the next room to execute their mission.

Epilogue

Later that night, as Howard and his family settled in back at home, he was changing and getting ready for bed when he found a note in his sport coat pocket. It read:

Howard,

It's me, Chuck. It was a pleasure getting to know you tonight. The world needs more men like you. Continue being the light in dark places. Anyway, I know you were wondering if angels really get their wings after completing a task like tonight's mission. We don't. We get something much better. A friend. Thank you for being my friend, Howard. I'll be seeing you around...get it? Guardian angel humor!

> *Yours truly,*
> *Chuck*

Ecclesiastes 11:1 - Invest what you have because after a while you will get a return.

> *P.S. I told you it was all about investments! See...it's even Biblical!*

Howard smiled as he placed the note in his nightstand. "Thanks again, Chuck," he said almost to himself. "Don't know if you can hear me or not, but I made a good friend tonight, too. See you around, buddy."

As Howard was making his way to the bedroom door to walk down the hall and join Molly and Heather in the family room, his radio alarm clock abruptly turned on by itself. Howard walked back to turn it off, only to hear *Monster Mash* suddenly playing from its speaker. Howard smiled even bigger this time as he decided to let it play. He turned off the light and left the room, knowing that the life he had always considered ordinary…was anything but.

Other Books by Jay W. Foreman

Still Learning

Bad Medicine:
Life Prescriptions from M.D. Hirschberg

Frontline Book 1: Tag…You're It

Frontline Book 2: Lost and Found

Raccoons' Christmas

How Christmas Saved The World From Aliens

Under The Sea Christmas Tree

A Calico Christmas

Our Thing

My Next Door Neighbor Is A Zombie

Benny The Bearded Bumble Bee

Mask Of The Monkey